Ravi's Rock Pool

Story by Cameron Macintosh

Illustrations by Gregor Forster

Contents

Chapter 1
Exciting News

"Good morning, class," said Ms Taranto. "I have some important news to tell you! This year's art show is all about the sea."

Ravi and the other children in his class were very excited.

"You have two weeks to make some artworks to put into the show," said Ms Taranto.

"I will paint a big blue whale!" said Nina.

"I'm going to make a huge turtle!" said Josh.

"And I will draw a picture of a rock pool on my tablet!" said Ravi.

Chapter 2

A Picture That Moves

At home that night, Ravi began to draw on his tablet.

He drew a rock pool in bright colours,
with plants, a clam, a crab and some other sea animals.

He held the tablet up and looked at it closely.

Ravi was proud of the picture he had drawn.

Later that week, Ravi looked at his picture again.

How can I make it even more special? he thought to himself.

"Maybe I'll make the plants and animals appear to move!" he said.

Using the controls on his tablet, Ravi made the plants move from side to side.
He made the clam open and close and the crab's legs move around.

"This looks great!" said Ravi.

He could hardly wait for the day of the art show.

Chapter 3

Setting Up for the Show

On the day of the art show,
Ms Taranto spoke to the class.
"I hope everyone is ready," she said.
"It's time to set up!"

Everyone went to the school hall with their artworks.

Ravi turned his tablet on, and stood it up on a desk.
He tapped on the screen,
and his plants and animals started moving.

Ravi looked around the hall.

Clara had made an oyster from two plastic plates.
Josh's turtle looked wonderful.
Erin had made a giant squid from paper and glue.
Nina had painted a big blue whale.
And in front of Ravi was a huge pink octopus made of cardboard.

Ravi looked down sadly at his tablet.
"No one will notice my tablet
among all of these big sea animals,"
he said to Nina.

"Is there a way we can make your rock pool bigger?"
asked Nina.

"I have an idea," said Ravi, suddenly.
"My plants and animals would look much better on a television screen."

Ravi ran over to Ms Taranto and told her his idea.

"Let's ask Mr Gill if we can use the television from the Year 6 room," Ms Taranto said.

Chapter 4

A Rock Pool on the Shore

A few minutes later, Ravi and Ms Taranto
moved the television into the hall
and put it on the desk.

Ravi turned on the television,
then tapped on his tablet.

Suddenly, the television screen
was full of Ravi's plants and animals.
"That looks wonderful!" said Ms Taranto.

But Ravi was disappointed.
"Something isn't quite right," he said.

"Why?" asked Ms Taranto.

"The television does not look like a rock pool,"
answered Ravi.

Ravi was quiet for a few seconds.
"I have an idea," he said.
"Nina and Josh, I need you to help me."

Ravi, Nina and Josh went out into the school garden.

"See those rocks over there?" said Ravi.
"Let's grab some and take them inside."

Ravi, Nina and Josh carried the rocks back into the hall.
Ravi placed the rocks on the desk, in front of the television.

"That's better!" he said, with a grin.
"Now it looks like a rock pool on the shore."

At 3 o'clock, everyone came to the art show.
They all loved Ravi's rock pool.

And no one was more surprised than Ravi, when Ms Taranto said he was the winner of the "Most Exciting Artwork" award!